GLUE

Constance Ann Fitzgerald

Lazy Fascist Press
PO Box 10065
Portland, OR 97296

www.lazyfascistpress.com

ISBN: 978-1-62105-227-2

Printed in the USA.

GLUE

For my parents Ray & Pat Fitzgerald—
stellar humans who taught me how to be human.

ONE

"The pool of blood was bigger than the motorcycle." The voice of your father's best friend, and vice president of the motorcycle club he founded, comes through the phone. He's shaken. He's a tough one. You know it's bad.

This is what you needed to hear yesterday to put you on an airplane. Yesterday his best friend's wife was assuring you that your father was up and about, ornery as ever. Demanding to be taken to a hotel and not the hospital. Your father hates hospitals.

He was adrenaline high, in shock, but bleeding out all over the pavement. That's the image you'll play back to yourself for months afterward. A pool of blood, your father's blood, seeping out around the edges of the machine that seems to be a fucking curse. All three accidents in the last several years, including the one that killed your mother, took place on the same bike and you want to roll it off a cliff into the ocean. Rot and rust, kill a thousand fish, but no more of your family.

You hang up and dial your brother. Apologize for not knowing how serious it was. Instead of saying "I'm on my way" you ask if you should be. He isn't going to tell you what to do, but it rings through.

You're needed there.

To support your brother and in case things get uglier.

You book the next flight out and call a friend to drive you to the airport. You can't quite focus to pack a bag. You don't know how long you'll be gone. Last time you were gone for weeks, ran out of clothes and had to buy more.

You stuff some t-shirts, jeans, and underwear into a backpack, and tell your coked-out roommate what's going on. Why you have to leave. She hates you, but you make her cry with tears streaming down your own crumpled face. She's awful but not heartless.

TWO

They were heading to Sturgis and they hadn't even made it out of the state when the truck in front of your father's motorcycle was cut off by a Cadillac that slammed on its brakes. The guys in the club and the VP's wife all say it with a sneer, "Cadillac." Like the driver thought he was above them simply by purchasing this vehicle. The driver of the Cadillac will swear up, down, and sideways that he stopped because of a sheep in the road. The driver of the truck and the people traveling with your father never saw any sheep. The Caddy cuts off the truck, the truck slams on its breaks so as not to hit the Caddy, and your father kisses the back of the truck. Kim, the VP's wife, will tell you about how she was right there behind him, frozen on her old man's bike, thinking *This is it. Not again.*

They'll all dismount and rush to your father, laying on the ground next to the guardrail, grey and sweating. He'll get up and shout "Goddamn it! Again? Fine. Take me to a fucking hotel!" and they'll tell him "No, you should really get to a hospital, brother."

And he won't listen until the paramedics show up or he loses consciousness.

Whichever comes first.

THREE

You had a lot of dreams about your father after your mom died. Some of them too close to real life for comfort.

You dreamed of him showing up on your front porch, belly swollen, hand in hand with someone who had already died. Ralph, your mom's father, held him upright at your door. In your kitchen your mom's mom was having tea at the table. Your mom, off screen, out of sight, in the laundry room. You can't see her but you know she's there because her presence radiates warmth and love. Your father enters the house and you pray that he and your mom's mom don't fight. They didn't get along when she was alive. She never understood the lifestyle and blamed your father when your little brother almost died in a car accident when the car he was in was struck by a drunk driver. Which had nothing to do with motorcycles.

Everyone in this dream, except you and your father, is dead in real life. Your mom's father died because he was a hundred years old. Stomach cancer and dementia. Then your mom in a motorcycle accident. Then her mom, probably because she just couldn't take it anymore.

In the dream, your father tells you he has something really important to say, something to tell you that he hasn't discussed with your mother yet. He says this and you realize that she's not there anymore and it hurts because she was just there and then she wasn't. Just like real life.

You never found out what it was that he wanted to tell you because he talked in circles about nothing until you woke up.

You called him a few days later and found out that he was going in for hernia surgery.

You dreamed of your father on his motorcycle, the oldest one, Georgia, named for the song "Georgia On My Mind." He's in the desert on a highway and the heat is radiating up from the pavement making waves on the horizon. His bike breaks down and he stumbles around, disoriented. In this dream he has a heart attack at the very same time that your mother dies. You wake yourself up sobbing because you'll never have another Dad Hug.

You're sure that it's going to bother him, calling every time you have a paranoid dream about his mortality.

So you wait.

When you call home he tells you about "testing" himself.

An endurance challenge because he's been off the bike too long. He wanted to see what kind of ride he could get in before he made a long haul for one of his conferences. His bike broke down between Phoenix and Tucson and it took two hours for someone to get to him. No water, no shade. He could barely walk by the time someone arrived. You convince yourself of a psychic connection to him. The way your brother can read your mind, you can see your father's future. It's reckless and bleak. And for a good man like him, it breaks your heart over and over and over and over and...

FOUR

Two years earlier, you were stoned at a Denny's in California with a girlfriend, eating something greasy and discussing something that seemed like a really big deal at the time. You were wrong.

Your phone rang and the caller ID said Kim with a little purple heart next to it. A longtime family friend, family herself, Kim never calls. Either she was stoned and thinking of you, in the area, or something was wrong. You felt it in the pit of your stomach. Your body always knows even when your mind doesn't.

"There's been an accident..." she says.

You go home and cry and make phone calls. Everyone tells you that your parents are unconscious in a Tennessee ICU.

You walk up to the corner store to buy a bottle of wine and you can't stop crying so the clerk rejects your purchase. He says your ID is fake. In reality you're a mess and he's trying not to be a part of it.

Back at your house there are a lot of your roommate's friends hanging out in the backyard skating the ramp. One of them goes to the store for you and buys you a bottle of wine. A better one than the one you picked out because she knows you're going to drink the whole thing so it may as well be quality.

Your brother calls you when he arrives at the hospital and tells you it's worse than they thought.

You check your bank account and know that there's no way in hell you can afford to get to Memphis on your own.

Your roommate hands you her credit card and tells you to do what you need to do.

While you're booking a flight online she rummages around in her bedroom and surfaces with one hundred and twenty-four dollars. It's all she has on her, and she hands it to you because you'll need cash to travel with. It's the single kindest thing anyone has ever done for you and you promise yourself that you'll pay her back somehow.

You never do.

FIVE

Sleep is a joke.

Your brain won't shut off or shut up. You drink a bottle of wine, smoke three bowls, and eat a cookie laced with marijuana. It helps you stop crying for a while, giving your raw eyes a break. You manage to lose consciousness for an hour. In the morning you head to the airport and you can't get there fast enough.

You change planes in Charlotte and are seated between an older man and woman. You try to order a whiskey and ginger ale but the flight attendant tells you they don't accept cash. The man sitting next to you talks to you for a few minutes. Asks if you are a student in Charlotte.

You tell him you aren't, you're from the Bay Area.

"What brings you out this way?"

You can't get further than "my parents" before your face dissolves into tears. You tell him. He tells you he's sorry, he'll pray for your family. He flags down the flight attendant and orders a double whiskey and ginger ale. When she brings it to him, he hands you the two novelty-sized bottles and the plastic cup of ginger ale.

"Don't drink it all at once," he says with a wink.

You pour one bottle into the cup, drink it halfway down and pour in the other.

The woman to your left opens a box of chocolate candies and offers them to you every time she takes one. She eats a few and hands you the rest of the box.

A couple of simple gestures that fill your broken heart with light.

You're terrified of flying. Every takeoff and every landing, you convince yourself that yours will be the plane that falls right out of the sky. You'll die screaming in a metal tube with hundreds of others until you burst into flames.

This time you're too preoccupied to worry about your own mortality.

When you get to Memphis it's late. You grab a cab and head straight to the hospital where your brother is waiting for you. He comes outside to greet you. He comes outside to warn you.

"Brace yourself. It's worse than you think it is."

The opposite of a pep talk, but wholly necessary. Steel yourself against what you're about to see. Try to.

There is no armor tough enough.

SIX

You go in to see your father first. He's beat to hell, but talking. He says your name and grabs your hand. Shaking it back and forth he looks at you and says, "Imma beat you up." Fighting back tears, you smile and tell him you'd like to see him try.

He's agitated and keeps asking you to help him up. He's gotta go.

The nurses suggest you head out, it's late and he needs rest.

You head up to see your mom. She's in the TICU, rigged up to every imaginable machine, and as the days pass she'll be hooked and unhooked to and from those machines. And more. They'll shave her head and you'll be in denial saying things like "She's gonna be mad about that when she wakes up." Because you still think she's going to wake up.

The next day you'll meet her biological son and daughter for the first time. There will be a veil of unification, family, until you get into the hotel room that night and her daughter asks how you're holding up. The shock will wear off and you'll fall apart right there, crying.

You'll say how awful this is, because you love your parents. You're so grateful for everything they have done for you. How perfect they are together. How happy you are that after the rough lives they've lived, they found each other.

How you're terrified of losing them and of them losing each other.

Your stepsister will sit on the bed across from yours and stare back at you until you're finished speaking/blubbering. She'll stand up and say, "I don't know about you, but both of *my* parents were drug addicts growing up." She'll walk to the bathroom and when she comes back out she'll put in some headphones and lay in bed with her back to you for the rest of the time you share a room.

There will be a day where your father asks you to tell his wife, your mom, that he loves her. Back in her room, you'll grasp her hand, hard to do when they say you can, hard not to when they ask you not to. You'll tell her your dad loves her, as you promised, and when you're walking down the corridor painted with images of the ER's namesake, Elvis, from floor to ceiling, your stepsister will stop you and ask you to limit the mentioning of your father because there are a lot of feelings and tensions floating around and it would be best if you just didn't talk about him.

You feel your fist clench.

You feel your arm begin to rise.

You have to fight the urge to sock her in the face with every ounce of strength you have left.

You say *okay* but you don't mean it.

Everyone is discussing what to do about dinner on the sidewalk outside the hospital and you tell them you aren't hungry and you're going up to your father's room to spend some time with him and maybe catch a nap. Your stepsister doesn't apologize and she doesn't speak to you for the remainder of her stay.

SEVEN

In the hotel in Tennessee, you were throwing yourself together before heading out with the rest of your tribe—family, friends, guys from your dad's club—back to the hospital.

You leaned into the mirror and swiped a mascara wand quickly through your lashes. Mostly out of habit.

But if you're honest, vanity factored in there too.

Your brother and stepsister were talking nearby and she looked over and said, "I didn't even *think* about bringing makeup."

Like you're some kind of asshole because you carry it in your purse.

After it's all over, whenever you think of her, you'll try to figure out exactly when she decided she hated you. Was it the first night in the hotel room you shared? Was it when you held your mom's hand and told her your father loved her, like you promised him you would, and she was too busy placing blame? Or was it before you'd ever actually met?

EIGHT

They insert a large metal rod in your mom's head called a "bolt," designed to relieve pressure. It seems counterproductive, and unsettling.

You walk into her room one day, and her hair is gone. Just that bolt jutting out from the side of her bald head.

No one called and asked.

No one warned you.

They'll take her to surgery and remove part of her skull to give her brain more room to swell.

Swell it does, right up against the skin flap of her scalp. Her whole body swells with fluids, skin straining and bloated, distorting her face and body.

The neurological team will refer to her injuries, her brain, as "angry." Which doesn't tell you much, but enough to know it isn't going to be good.

You sit in the waiting room for hours, wrecked and nauseated with nerves while they cut out sixty percent of her brain.

NINE

Everyone else goes home and you and your little brother corner a neurosurgeon in your mom's hospital room, ask him to level with you. He points at her in the hospital bed, bucking and fighting the ventilator, being pumped and drained.

"That's it. That's her for the rest of her life," he says.

And you and your brother know you have to let her go.

The two of you go back to your hotel room and kill the last of the beers floating in melted ice in the bathroom sink. You're sitting on hotel room bedspreads, staring down at the geometric pattern and trying not to feel anything. Your stomach is in knots so you force each beer down, gagging with every swallow.

You and your brother were lucky enough to meet a nice guy in the room next to yours who hooks you up with a joint after overhearing some of your brother's telephone conversation on the shared deck.

A day later your brother talks to the guy and says he hates to ask, but does he have any more weed? The guy hands him a fistful of roaches and says it's all he's got, but you and your brother probably need it more than he does.

Your brother goes to the gas station and gets you an apple so you can stab a ballpoint pen through it a couple of times and MacGuyver it into a pipe.

You smoke some weed out of the apple, drink as much beer as your stomach will allow. You manage to get a few words out without dissolving into sobs. You used to be so fucking strong, but you find yourself crying every time you try to speak. Your little brother just drapes a skinny arm around your shoulders and lets you cry.

He tells you it will be okay.

He's seven years younger than you, but he's the rock and you feel like calling him your "little" brother is an insult to the man he is.

"If the machines have been what's keeping her alive this whole time, I guess she really died a week ago," you say.

You expect your brother to be sort of angry at the statement for some reason. But he isn't. He takes another swig from his beer and nods.

You called your aunt, crying into the phone, "We need an adult." And with that she was on her way.

The decision was made, unanimously, it was time to let your mom go. Your mother and father had the conversation a thousand times.

Neither of them wanted to be vegetables. Neither of them wanted to live that way. Because to them it wasn't living at all.

Everyone, your mother included, just assumed that if it happened at all, it would be your father.

TEN

Your brother will wake you up the morning it's supposed to happen. The official letting go. The morning they are going to unplug all the machines and set her free.

You can't get out of bed. Your body is heavy and your eyes refuse to open. You struggle to wake up and your body fights back.

You don't want to be awake for this.

You force yourself up and out of bed. You wedge yourself between the bathtub and the toilet of the small hotel bathroom and vomit for half an hour, your body's automatic reaction to stress. You crawl back into bed because you don't know what else to do.

Your brother walks to the gas station on the corner to get you a ginger ale, but all they have is

Sprite. He hands it to you and tells you it's time to get up. Your grandmother bought you plane tickets out of Tennessee and your flight leaves soon.

Your aunt, a registered nurse, is going to handle the ugly business of letting your mother go. She says you and your brother have been tormenting yourselves enough watching her in the hospital room, you don't need to see this too.

You hunker down in the bathroom again, a grown ass woman hiding from her aunt. You smoke a couple roaches out of the puckered and brown apple before stuffing your belongings back into your backpack.

Your brother crams your mother's helmet, which the hospital wrapped in a hazmat bag to contain any "organic debris," into the duffel bag he bought and you call a cab.

In Charlotte, North Carolina, you rush through the airport past gigantic white rocking chairs to catch your connecting flight, which has already boarded.

The airline gave your seats away because they didn't think you'd make it.

"Our mom is dying and we're just trying to get home," your brother says.

The girl at the desk apologizes and boards

the plane. When she returns, she has a father and daughter trailing behind her. Where most people would be angry, they look at you and your brother with sad and sympathetic eyes.

Seeing that this works, a man also trying to board the flight says, "Yeah, me too. My mom has cancer and only has twenty-four hours to live."

They don't believe him, and they shouldn't, but they make the adjustment and allow him to board after you're already seated. The man passes your brother in the aisle and your brother shoots daggers at him while the liar tries desperately to avoid eye contact, knowing he's the scum of the earth.

ELEVEN

Your dad is a political legend in the motorcycle community. He was elected to represent all of the clubs in the nation. They chose him, feeling that he had everyone's best interests at heart because he wanted them all to enjoy the same rights. He also wanted them all to get along and stop killing each other.

Three times a year he runs workshops across the country to talk to them about just that.

This year your mother joined him and on their way to one in North Carolina they caught some bad weather in Memphis, Tennessee. While trying to get around a semi-truck, they didn't see that the traffic in the other lane had stopped.

The rain made it even more difficult to stop.

They managed to cut their speed down by

about half before they went down. So as not to slam into the back of another vehicle, your dad uses his years of experience and lays it down flat, trying to ride it out.

The asphalt was wet and the bike flipped, bucking and smashing them into the road. They had just put on their helmets.

Your dad is generally opposed to helmets. He fights those laws too, believing that it should be the individual's right and not enforced by the state. You respect that. When you let The Man take one right away, you open them up to take away more rights, until you have none. There are helmet laws in some states that force folks to wear helmets. Your parents had some ADOT approved shells that resembled helmets but offered no real protection. Really just so they wouldn't get pulled over.

A real helmet would have taken the same amount of effort to wear. A lot of head injuries are caused from the brain colliding with the skull, from the inside.

There is no real safety.

Your dad had six hemorrhages down the center of his brain. Three on each side in a bloody little row. He fractured his face and several ribs, broke his collar bone, shoulder blade, and punctured a lung.

For the first two days his head injuries had him convinced that all of the nurses in the hospital were cops. That they had all shown him their badges when he asked to see them and that your mom was being locked up and used against him in a political ploy.

Part head injury and maybe part something inside him trying to deny the truth: that the woman he loved, his wife of twenty years, and without a fucking question the love of his life, was in far worse shape than he was. Now his, and everyone's, worst fear has come to life: that she wouldn't make it. **You try to ask yourself** why, but it's futile.

You're flying to Arizona from Memphis without your mom.

TWELVE

Your friend introduced you to a guy and the two of you hit it off. You're awkward as hell so he really had to work to get to you.

But he did.

Three days later you and your friend were pulling his body out from the driver's seat of her boyfriend's car while his mouth turned yellow, green, and then blue.

The four of you had woken up early considering how late you'd stayed up drinking the night before. His bedroom window didn't have any curtains and the sunlight streamed through and bounced off the bare walls and white comforter on the bed, blinding you the second you opened your eyes.

The two of you walked down the block on a

coffee run and he told you about his sister and his mother and what the plan was for the day. The four of you would be going out to Stafford Lake for a mini music festival.

You spent the day in the sunshine, drinking cheap beer and eating marijuana-laced foods from people who wandered around the lake shouting about their edibles for sale.

Walking back to the car, he will reach for your hand and you'll inch away. Because nice guys make you nervous and that's why every "relationship" you've ever had is a fucking travesty.

You and your friend will climb and contort into the back seat of her boyfriend's sports car, and her boyfriend will get in on the passenger side and his friend will pull the car out of the parking lot and say he hopes he doesn't get pulled over because he's high as shit.

Which wasn't really any different from any other day.

You won't get far before you're going around a large curve and he lets out a small low chuckle.

"Ha."

He'll lean over like he's looking at the stereo and the car will start to veer into oncoming traffic. Your friend's boyfriend will look over and say,

"Hey, man. Keep your eyes on the road," before realizing that he isn't just fucking around with the music. He's slumped over like a fucking rag-doll behind the wheel of the car.

On instinct he'll reach out and steer the car around the curve, and beach it on the grassy shoulder a few yards ahead. You scream the whole time. Your friend is pre-med and climbs up on to the center console the second the car is stopped to check him out. You and her boyfriend get out of the car. Her boyfriend is catatonic and she asks you to help her get the driver out onto the ground, flat, so she can perform CPR.

"I can't," you'll say.

She'll tell you you don't have a choice and that she needs your help.

So you nut up and do it.

She'll unhook his seat belt and you each grab an arm and drag him out onto the asphalt. You're trying to call for help, but with the trees and valleys you can't get a signal on your cell. You start flagging down cars as they pass.

It's amazing how many look right at you and keep driving.

Finally someone stops and they have reception. They call 911 and the paramedics arrive. Your friend talks to them with their medical jargon and you stand on the opposite side of the car with her boyfriend. You can't stop staring.

You watch the EMT with feathery white hair perform chest compressions. You watch his head flutter up and down behind the car until your friend's boyfriend grabs you by the shoulder and makes you turn away. You face the chain link fence and stare at the dandelions creeping through until the ambulance pulls away without lights or sirens.

You sat in that bleak little waiting room next to the ER for hours and when someone finally comes to talk to you it's the coroner. He asks if Andrew was chewing gum at the time and you'll swallow the half a piece still in your mouth. The other half apparently lodged in his throat during some form of cardiac arrest brought on because of his enlarged heart that he was unaware of.

You get dropped off at your apartment. You text your boss and give her the CliffNotes version of what happened.

You were in a car.

The driver died in front of you.

You won't be coming in to work.

You collapse into bed and stay there until Sarah shows up with her dog, chocolate cupcakes, and vodka.

Uneasy, you'll call home. Your mom will tell you about "Survivor's Guilt" and make you promise not to get swept up in it. That it doesn't help anyone. It doesn't bring them back.

You know she is right, but it doesn't go away.

A couple of years later, when she dies, there won't be anyone to call for sage advice. You'll try to remember her words, think of what she would have said. You know she'd want you to be strong. Live your life.

But it's hard and you need a fucking drink.

THIRTEEN

After your parents' accident, you sleep at the foot of your dad's bed like a dog. You give him space and stay as still as humanly possible so as not to agitate or disturb the sleep he thinks he's not getting. He's got a ton of broken bones so you don't want the mattress to shift under your weight. When you eventually drift off, that's when he needs to get up to use the bathroom and you have to get up and plant your feet into the ground next to his side of the bed to hoist him up.

Nighttime, when everything goes quiet and there's no one left to talk to, is when you want to cry. But you don't want your father to hear it, or feel your body shuddering next to him. You save it for the shower, when you're alone and you can claim soap in your eyes if anyone asks afterward.

You don't sleep for a week.

FOURTEEN

There's a point after you get home, when it's all over and it starts to sink in, where all you can do is think about how long it's been since you were home for a visit. Years. You had excuses, all of them financial. But what really held you back was pride. That ugly fuck. You're not good at asking for help. But that's all you had to do. You could have called home and said, "I'd like to come visit you but I can't really afford it. Can we split the cost?" Or at some points in your financial roller coaster, just an open-ended "Could you help me out?" She would have. But you couldn't, didn't. Because you could do Thanksgiving/Christmas next year.

Now there wasn't going to be a next year.

You crawl into bed. Complete silence and then ringing. Horrible, anxiety-inducing ringing. You play music. Something to focus on. It fades into the melody. You cannot stand silence. You finally drift off but wake only a couple hours later with a pain in your head like someone trying to escape using an ice pick. You roll around in bed, cry and say, "No, please. Make it stop. No, no, no!"

It eventually passes. You fall asleep out of sheer exhaustion and never really know what caused it.

FIFTEEN

You called and made all the arrangements for your mom's cremation. Your grandmother paid for it. Over a thousand dollars.

Your dad doesn't tell you when her remains arrive. You only know they finally did because your brother talks about riding out to the place her ashes were scattered and spending time in "her place."

Maybe your father forgot, because of his head injuries.

Maybe he didn't think you wanted to know, which you did.

Maybe he was angry because you couldn't stay any longer and had to get back to your job and home to pay rent and get back to work.

You'd been gone for almost two months. You wanted to stay, but everyone, your brother and aunt included, told you you'd done all you could. Go home. Get to work. Pay your bills. Attempt to replenish your bank account. Live your life.

The thought that maybe your father was mad sticks with you. Mad may not be the right word, disappointed might be. There's a huge part of you that felt you should have stayed. You should have dropped your life and moved back home to help out and take care of your father. But everyone told you not to. That it wasn't what was best for you or your life plan and you'd regret it. There's a part of you that feels like maybe your father resents that, but you'll never ask. He isn't someone who generally talks about feelings.

And even if you could get him to talk this time, what he might say could kill you where you stand.

SIXTEEN

Your father and brother scattered her ashes in the same place she married your father. A cliff around Wolf Creek that looks out onto the forest.

You have a photo of their wedding day; her in an old fashioned high collared lacy dress and white cowboy boots. Your father in a suit with a bolo tie. The only kind of tie you've ever seen him wear.

Another photo from the reception, held in their living room, where your mom is holding a slice of cake in the air toward your father and he's smiling and you can see the objection on his face. He knows she's going to smash the cake into his beard. They look at each other like teenagers in love, and that's the same way they look at each other for the next twenty years.

There are days when you feel lonely and wholly unlovable. Those days, you try to think of their love. The awful relationships they both endured before they found each other, in their mid-thirties attending recovery meetings.

SEVENTEEN

There is a night you can't sleep. A realization keeps you awake: Someday you're going to have to do this all over again. How else would your father leave this world, if not on a motorcycle? He won't stop, and you'd never ask him to. He's suffered many head injuries. How many until his body gives up and out? What if he dies? Worse, what if he's just a drooling mess? He'd loathe it.

"What if he dies?" That's the one that keeps you awake. Because it isn't if, it's when. It will happen someday. Your superhuman father is a *human*. And that's what sent you over the edge. Thrown over a waterfall of your own tears in a barrel, like that would save you. You realized that someday your father will die and you'll feel this awful unyielding blackness all over again. A thought you couldn't bear, high as the devil, alone in the dark: Someday your father won't be around. You pray that it happen *years* from now. Because you can't ask for it to never come. It's impossible and certainly something your father would never want.

A moment of clarity that shone through the dramatics of your breaking/broken heart: Someday your dad will die. Any number of scenarios are possible, but with his heart condition and passion for two wheels meeting two lanes, you're guessing it's one of the two. Would fate really be so cruel? Could you and your brother really have to go through it all again? Maybe you'd be more prepared because you've already done it once. Because you know what he'd want you to do.

It wouldn't be any easier. You hated the thought but you couldn't shut it off. It spun circles around you, not letting you sleep. What of your fractured family then? You thought about how your brother was so upset that your mom would never meet his kids, her would-be grandchildren. Your father likely would. Your brother and his high school sweetheart got engaged shortly after your mom passed. It was only a matter of time for them. Not so much for you.

You know your father is proud of you. You know your mom would be too. But you'd like to do and be more for the both of them. For yourself. You don't want him to worry. You want to be happy, but you're miserable and drinking too fucking much. He'd hate that.

You'll do things you know are bad for you. Things you know won't end well. In the moment you'll rationalize it into something passable. Or you'll shrug it off in two simple words: "fuck it." Because you've stopped caring. About everything. Especially yourself.

Which isn't entirely true.

In fact, you care deeply for everything. Except yourself. Because it just doesn't seem to matter anymore. You'll drink until you can't see straight, lurching and retching in the morning and well into the afternoon. Cold sweat in a film all over your body, you'll lay on the bathroom floor for the cool comfort of the tile until you're too sleepy to keep your eyes open. At some point your roommate will need to use the bathroom.

You'll crawl back to bed, call into work, and smoke a bunch of pot before the next wave of nausea hits so you can fall asleep for the rest of the day. You'll want to say this is the last time, at least for a while. But you know better. You're a lot of things, but a liar isn't one of them.

If your dad knew how often you did this, that it was how you cope, he'd be pissed. And worse yet, disappointed. His shining alcoholic star, so desperate for comfort that she'll drown herself.

Sake, tequila, beer, tequila, wine, sangria, beer, Fernet, Fernet, Fernet, beer, Fernet. On a Monday. It's a slippery slope. You'll try not to get swallowed up.

But you won't make any promises.

EIGHTEEN

Your father is in a hospital bed again. His face shaved and tubes stuffed down his throat, like your mom's almost exactly two years ago. He can't speak so he pantomimes at you vigorously to give him a glass of water. You can't because he'll choke on it.

When he's taken off the ventilator and able to breathe on his own, he'll yell at you because he wants his black Levi's, and you can't give them to him because it isn't time to go home yet and they cut his pants off after the accident anyway.

He's mad.

Not at you. Just in general. But it feels like it is at you because those are the words that are coming out.

You know better, but it hurts anyway. You

learned, between the two accidents in as many years, that you would be willing to do irreparable damage to yourself if you thought you were helping the people you loved.

Once, the nurses asked him who the people in the room were—your brother, his wife, and you.

"That's my son, his wife, and my ex."

Because he thought you were your biological mother. Someone you are less than fond of.

Another day, when he wasn't able to speak because he was intubated, he held your hand and squeezed it tight when you told him you loved him. He turned your hand over and tapped on the turquoise ring on your ring finger. Because it was your mom's and he'd probably given it to her. How that made you hopeful. Hopeful that maybe you'd get your dad back.

You're not blind to the future.

If that's how he wants to go out, that's what's going to happen. No bleeding or pleading will change that because from his hospital bed, staples holding his scalp together in the back, he stares across the room and says, "I'm looking forward to going for a ride."

NINETEEN

It's two hours from your dad's house to the hospital where he's laid up. Your brother usually makes it in forty-five minutes to an hour. Your brother hates all of your music but he lets you play it because he knows it's something else for you to focus on. A way to pretend to calm down in two or three minute spurts. You have a few classic rock songs saved. Ones that make you think of your parents. Ones that make you think of home.

"Midnight Rider" comes on, and the air gets sucked from the cab of the truck. Your brother focuses hard out the windshield and mouths the words to the song. The hard lump rises from the pit of your stomach and locks in your throat. You try to swallow it. Try to steady your quivering lip.

TWENTY

Your father's body temperature is sky high and they can't keep it down. One of many parts of his brain that are injured, the part that regulates his body temperature, has a bleed. They give him Tylenol, surround him with ice packs and fill his room with electric fans. They do their best to keep him comfortable, but all he wants to do is leave.

Back in Memphis that's exactly what he did.

Convinced a couple of his buddies that he was discharged, unhooked himself from tubes and monitors, hopped in the truck and bolted. The drive from Tennessee to Arizona nearly killed him. Somewhere along the road he had visions of your mother, telling him to be strong and stick it out for the kids. That you needed him.

This time around everyone is on notice: no one takes him anywhere without explicit orders from the doctors or your brother. He spends most of his time hollering to leave, that he has things to do and places to be. He tugs at the tubes stuffed down his throat and the IVs in his arm. He swings his legs over the side of the bed, tries to sit up, but the pain from his broken collar bone, scapula and several broken ribs usually slows him down. He'll reach out and say, "Help me up, I'm goin' that way." He'll point at the door and try to make his escape. While he's intubated they'll strap his arms down. After a while they'll have someone come sit in the room with him because he can't be left alone without shouting or attempting escape. You and your brother just seem to agitate him, because he knows he's the boss and the two of you won't do, can't do, what he's asking.

He'll be transferred between hospitals and rehabilitation centers teeming with old folks. After two months they'll let him go home with the promise that he'll be under constant supervision. Which he won't, so much as there will be a revolving door of friends taking turns caring for him.

One night he'll make less sense. He'll regress enough to cause alarm and your aunt will make someone take him to the hospital where they'll find that his brain is bleeding again. He'll stay overnight and in the morning he'll unhook himself from various machines, pull on his pants and walk out the door, tired of being held against his will.

He'll go some back way, over the creek, stepping on slick wet stones to cross. Endangering himself because of his lack of balance and still healing bones. They'll find him wandering around near the pawn shop after a few hours and bring him home.

TWENTY-ONE

A story your father told you where he used to chug tequila to get out of bed in the morning. One of those guys where you can't tell just how intoxicated they are because their demeanor never really changes. Prompting his friends to nickname him "Still Ray" because he was always the same guy.

Once when you asked your mom why they called him that, she told you it was because he showed up at someone's house and the girl who answered the door was so fucked up that when he came back the following night she opened the door, stared at him, turned back to the rest of the group and said, "It's *still* Ray." Losing track of time, moments, thinking he was just perpetually knocking on their door. A purgatory where he never gets to cross the threshold and she's just a doorman. You guess that was better than telling you what an awful drunk he used to be.

It was his feeling that all of his mistakes, and the fact that he was an alcoholic, a thief, and an addict, were not useful to his parenting. Strictly things he could discuss once you and your brother were adults.

He told you that when he quit drinking it was because he came out of a blackout on his motorcycle in the middle of the desert. He left his bike in the sand to hike up a hill and see where the fuck he was. Ended up on the backside of a California restaurant chain. He began his bender somewhere around Vegas, where he lived at the time.

He got his bearings, and his bike, and ventured home. At the time he lived in a house by a golf course. He got home, told his then-wife that he was leaving and she could have everything except his motorcycle, and left.

Years later she lost the house. She only needed a couple thousand to be able to keep it. Trying to make peace, your father offered her the money. No strings attached. Just an apology. Good will. A penance.

So full of hate, she'd rather lose the house, which she did, than accept his money. Somewhere between the time he left and the time he offered her money, he came to visit his oldest daughter and his stepson. His stepson had a lot of issues and a lot of anger. He also had a parrot who would perch on his forearm and when prompted would attack the person he was gestured toward. Knowing this, your father stood in the living room talking to his estranged family and when his stepson pointed the bird toward your father, your father pulled out his pistol and shot it out of the air. An explosion of feathers and bird guts strewn across the carpet.

He tells this story, deadpan. He finishes it by plainly stating, "I was asked to leave."

He has a way of telling outrageous stories as though they are nothing. Legendary, superhuman tales of his life that he shrugs off, but the little sparkle in his eye tells you he gets a kick out of the reaction.

You used to make him tell the story of the time he was bitten by the brown recluse because you loved how calm his voice was when he talked about cutting into his stomach, with the pocket knife that was always strapped to his hip, to remove the dead tissue he had packed drywall mud into. The matter-of-fact tone of his response when, eyes wide, you'd ask, "Didn't that HURT?!?"

"Only when you hit the parts that are still alive." Like it was nothing at all.

When he was detoxing and he needed a project, he built you a dollhouse. He glued each tiny pebble individually to the chimney. The plan was to finish it with you. To pick out miniature furniture and dolls together. He dropped it off at your grandmother's house and she tucked it away in the craft room where you were not allowed to go. Being a child who rarely obeyed orders, you wandered in and found it. You asked what it was and she said it was a project of hers. It disappeared shortly after, most likely thrown in the garbage.

He'd come by the house to visit you and your biological mother would go outside and take all the tools from the saddlebags on the bike, throw them up and down the street and into bushes, then call the cops and tell them that he wouldn't leave the property.

TWENTY-TWO

One of your dad's friends says it online after your mom's service: "She was with us and made her presence known."

He goes on to talk about a red-tailed hawk and a significance that doesn't quite resonate with you. An anecdote about maturity. Despite the hawk, he isn't wrong. There was a point when Ralo, the woman asked to host the service for the family, gestured toward a table filled with flowers and photographs of your mom. She said the mourners were free to browse them, but please don't take them home. Your family didn't have doubles.

Some of these were photos you don't think your mom would have liked very much. Besides her generally being critical of herself in photos the way so many women are, you remember going through boxes of photographs in the living room and picking out which ones would be used for the service. Ralo held one for a second and showed it to you.

"This one. She looks beautiful."

She did. She was young and smiling, glowing. And almost naked.

You shook your head no. Inappropriate.

She showed your brother and his eyes widened for a second before he said, "I don't think she would appreciate us showing everyone that picture. I'm pretty sure it was supposed to be private." You tucked it into another box, buried it underneath more photos.

The morning of the service it was sunny and warm. The weather was perfect for riding. There was a moment when Ralo told everyone to look at the photos, that you looked up and the sky was just a little grey, and a big gust of wind blew the photos off the table and swirling onto the ground.

Right then.

That's when you felt her.

And you laughed and it felt good and you wished you were better at public speaking.

TWENTY-THREE

You're a hopeless romantic. Falling in love at the drop of a hat with anyone foolish enough to be attractive and kind to you. It's become a problem. Always heartbroken or in the process of breaking.

It's exhausting.

You're a giant open wound that can't manage to heal. Sometimes it gets close and you just keep bumping into things and tearing it open. You can't help but pick at it. None of it sanitary. None of it comfortable.

Think of the heart like an antique vase. A Ming vase, or whatever that fancy expensive shit is. It's that.

You're clumsy, but you've decided that the vase looks so nice on that spindly carved table next to your front door where you drop your keys in the dark after you've unlocked the door. Before you turn on the lights. What you ought to have is one of those sturdy Victorian card tables your archaeologist roommate told you about. The ones where people leave calling cards then you decide whether or not you want to see them once they've already called on you.

When you come home drunk at night, or exhausted from your third double shift in as many days, you flop your hand outward, your fingers graze that precious pottery and knock it to the ground.

"Shit," you slur as you bend down, collect all the tiny fragments and leave them on the kitchen table to superglue back together in the cold sober light of morning.

Again.

You'll squint at the edges, trying to puzzle piece it all back together, matching up broken edges and patterns. Attempting perfect placement and trying to hide that it ever suffered an impact.

That it ever belonged to you.

Each time this happens the ritual is less effective. It fractures in different places. Smaller pieces get lost and you have to crawl under the couch to seek them out. Some break into such fine pieces that they turn to dust, leaving large gaps that you try to just fill up with more glue.

Getting older feels this way.

In your teenage years and early twenties you bounced back. Maybe not very quickly, but eventually. You'd fill yourself with hate, point and shoot until the person you'd been hurt by no longer existed to you. You'd forget them.

It feels like aging slows down the pace of healing. The same way our bones were softer, more malleable, as children. In the Golden Years, there are steel hips and knee joints because eventually our bodies give out on us. Misuse—or hell, existing at all—leads to damage.

You thought you'd felt true sadness. In fact, you were almost addicted to it. You'd write poems and essays brooding about autumn's beauty and finding a beauty in death that wasn't there.

Your father read one such essay when you were in high school and sighed as he set down the paper.

"Why do you always write about death? There's nothing beautiful about it. You don't know what you're talking about."

You found this offensive because seventeen-year-olds know everything.

He was right.

You'd never seen anyone die before. Slowly or brutally, it was foreign to you. You'd read a lot of Plath. It was different in real life.

When you watched Andrew die that sunny afternoon you knew exactly what your father meant. There was nothing beautiful about it. You stood horrified and you couldn't look away until your friend's boyfriend physically turned you away from the scene. You stood with your back to the road staring vacantly at yellow dandelions growing through a chain link fence. They swayed in the cool evening breeze and you said to yourself, over and over, "He'll be okay. He's fine. They'll bring him back. He'll be okay…" until they loaded him up in the ambulance and drove away without sirens or lights.

You see those little yellow lions in the grass everywhere, springing up between squares of concrete, and you cringe. Every time. Little yellow weeds that haunt you with a memory that you want to bury somewhere it can never crawl out of. It sticks in your mind like the brilliance of the sunshine reflected off his comforter and bare white walls that morning. So bright that you had to cover your face until you shambled out of bed.

The coroner came into that little waiting room in the ER. He said hello and asked if Andrew was chewing any gum at the time of his death. You cheeked the half a piece of gum you had been gnawing on all afternoon. The other half was what they thought obstructed his breathing. The coroner nodded and said nothing. You swallowed your gum.

In second grade a teacher's aide saw you swallow your gum. She knelt down and poked her finger into your sternum, something your biological mother did when she was angry, so you flinched. She saw you recoil and smiled brightly.

"When you swallow your gum it gets stuck right here," she said, tapping gently on your chest. "For seven years."

You told Juliana about Andrew's gum. Not that you swallowed it, just that it was brought up. That you were chewing the other half of it.

"Did you save it?"

You stared at her.

"I'm a creep. I would have saved it," she said.

"I swallowed it."

"You swallowed it?! That shit takes YEARS to digest."

"I know."

She gave you a hug and bought you another drink.

It changed so much. You thought you'd never see something so traumatic in your lifetime. How could you? You woke up in his bed the last two mornings and by the end of that day, early evening, he was dead.

You cried for a month.

It would just wash over you sometimes. If you sat in the backseat on the passenger side of a car and you felt the car was going too fast, you'd have panic attacks.

You've had dreams for years about being in a car that has no driver. Sometimes it was clear to you that you were supposed to be driving from the backseat. It smacked of symbolism.

Take hold of your life. Get some fucking direction.

After Andrew's death those dreams seemed much more literal. You didn't think anything could top it until you got that call from a family friend telling you that your parents had been in an accident.

TWENTY-FOUR

When your mom died it was complicated. You spent a solid week thinking that just maybe she would wake up and be herself again.

By a week and some change you realized she'd need to be cared for, she wouldn't remember you or your family, or have any kind of creativity or problem solving skills. She'd be a shell of the amazing woman she once was.

A day or so later, you and your little brother cornered a neurosurgeon who pointed at her, wired and stuffed with tubes leaking or pumping fluids and forcing her to breathe, and said, "This is probably going to be her for the rest of her life."

When you got home, before the funeral, you took the leather jacket she was wearing during the accident, the jacket she died in, and shredded it. You braided pieces of it with blue ribbon, attached it to key-rings, tied it in knots, left big chunky pieces in a box, and saved a large enough piece to make a forearm cuff for your father. The small, braided and knotted pieces were handed out at her service so everyone could wear them, tie them to their colors or bikes, or just hold them. It's a slightly morbid but lovely tradition.

You wear yours like a bracelet and let the leather and ribbons dangle when you walk. You fiddle with the tassels in your sleeve. You rub the leather between your index finger and thumb. You took her other leather jacket out of your parents' closet and wore all winter long to keep out the wind and to feel close to her.

True heartbreak is watching your mother fight the machines keeping her alive. Seeing her there for almost two weeks and then realizing it wasn't going to get better. Watching your father, through his head injury and medicated fog, you see a flicker of recognition. How he realized she wasn't just asleep when she didn't wake up as he grasped her hands and said, "Hey, my girl. You sleepin'?"

Since that break nothing can heal. Maybe that's why you just can't seem to care about anything right now. Why everything and everyone seems totally trivial and useless.

TWENTY-FIVE

Around the time your grandmother was dying, you had to go to a convention for a long weekend. You decided to "quit" drinking. Or at least take a leave of absence. The last year had been rough and it wasn't getting any easier. You spent most of it as drunk as possible. Every so often you'd think about how pissed your dad would be about your consumption. Or worse, how disappointed your mom would be if she were still alive.

You decided that the only way to avoid being a huge fucking mess was to not make it an option. Emotional, sure. Shit happens, but you weren't going to be that train wreck that you have a tendency to be. You holed up with some friends who don't drink, hung out with people who cheered you up and took your mind off things, and got through the weekend with minimal scenes made. When you got home you didn't want to go sit on a bar stool in the same bar you'd been hanging out in for seven years.

Somewhere in there something clicked and you realized you're not a good drunk. A lot of your stories involve you vomiting for hours or being a less literal mess. Either way, you're not good at alcoholism.

TWENTY-SIX

You're lying in bed with all the lights out. Just the space age flashing of lights across the television. You're watching *Star Trek*. You're watching this old Vulcan's control deteriorate with age and thinking, "Nothing ever lasts."

You're watching Geordi La Forge and thinking how lonely this poor blind bastard is, that he should only find companionship on the Holodeck.

And how you kind of wish you had a Holodeck.

When you were a kid, you used to wear headbands across your eyes and pretend to be him, and you weren't sure why.

Deanna Troi was so pretty.

This poor blind bastard. (Your head hurts; where are your glasses?)

When you were a child, playing make-believe aboard your own personal star ship, floating around your grandmother's living room, you'd cover your eyes and shoot pretend phasers. Once, you used a slap bracelet as a make-shift visor. Those strips of metal you lash at your wrists with, and all it does is coil around the bone. Maybe with a little spin and sparkle. Not yours. Yours had been a pink satin, and you'd worn it until it was stained brown. You half deployed it and put it across your eyes, when it snapped and scraped quickly to its coil shape, while you froze. Horrified. Seeing perfectly well, but certain blindness would come on at any second.

These ideas and fears weren't anything new to you. Not even at six. You were always falling down on or near something sharp, and paralyzed until you realized you were nearly alright. You'd scraped your knees, and stapled thumbs, bruised shins, and bitten off pieces of your cheek in your sleep.

And you were surviving just fine without special assistance from space age science.

TWENTY-SEVEN

Your mother taught you a good many things. She wanted to impress upon you the way the world worked, and how you should work in it. How to survive in it. All based on her own experiences or experiences from the people she knew and had watched flail and fail through life.

In a club your father used to belong to, a lot of the guys had started using drugs and screwing around on their wives or girlfriends. This naturally angered her. Because those women were her friends. But also because, no matter how much she trusted your father, this was the company he kept.

She picked you up from school one day and you don't recall how you got on the topic, but she let you know that the general idea/ideal of love was bullshit. That all the swooning and passion weren't real love so much as they were lust and hormones. That real love was something simpler. It was trust, friendship, and respect.

She said that if your father ever did anything like those other guys, she'd tell him to leave, and she'd be keeping the kids. Both of you. Because even though she wasn't your biological mother, she still thought of you as hers.

You both got misty eyed then, and you knew you finally had a mother.

TWENTY-EIGHT

Right before you moved into the house where you live, the woman who lived across the street was in her car and had a cardiac event in which her car rolled back up onto the sidewalk and hit a tree. She bled out and died right there in front of her house before the paramedics could reach her. Her family took to making that tree a happy place. A memorial for someone they love deeply. There were balloons, half buried vases overflowing with flowers, stuffed animals, and a photo of her, Mary, beaming with the kind of light that only comes from on high.

When you and your friend were unloading your belongings from the moving van, Mary's family came out and talked to you. They said that if you lived there you were family now. They invited you to her service and the candle light vigil on the street in front of her home.

Mary's loved ones started to gather around six or seven o' clock. From your new bedroom window you had an amazing view of their vigil, but couldn't quite hear all of the people speaking and sharing their fond memories of Mary. Even with your window open. You went out to the front porch to listen and it stopped raining, so you joined the edge of the crowd that gathered and blocked the street.

They spoke of her as a woman who was always there to help. A woman with an abundance of love for everyone she met. A woman who had made mistakes in her life, gone down a really dark path, and then decided she wanted more for herself. So, she went out and got it.

She and your mom had a lot in common.

You did not know this woman. You had only ever met the photo of her at the base of the tree, opposite the pool of blood in the soil where she died, but you stood out on the sidewalk and cried with her family and friends. You knew what they were feeling because you'd been there too.

They talked about how Mary had died once already. She was resurrected. A car accident that landed her in a coma, where she miraculously recovered.

Your mind flashed back to the first time you were trying to make sense of why your mom couldn't pull through, why she was gone. At that time a little voice in your head told you that she had already had her second chance, when she got down on her knees and prayed to make a better life for herself, at a time when she wasn't quite the stellar woman you knew.

A young woman got up and belted out a song you had never heard before.

It sounded like gospel. She sang that all of Mary's troubles and trials were over now.

You felt your mom there with you, in a crowd of strangers, mourning a woman who was gone before you arrived, and you felt comforted then.

Everything just might be okay.

When you went back up to your room you lit a candle and placed it in the window closest to the vigil. It wasn't until you lay down that you realized you lit the Saint Stevie Nicks candle your old roommate made for you. You fell asleep thinking about riding through the desert listening to "Rumors" on the cassette deck in your mom's truck. You think of her staring out the windshield, singing along to "You Make Lovin' Fun" with the desert sun shining on her face.

She drove too fast, but you were never afraid.

Thanks and love to:

Tom Fitzgerald, Joann Serracino, Erin Conway, Jay Dee Fillingim, Terry and Kim Bobo, the Fitzgerald clan, Sarah Elkins, Rios De La Luz, Tiffany Scandal, Meliza Bañales, Laura Lee Bahr, Cameron Pierce, J David Osborne, Jessica Standifird, Sally K Lehman, Rhiannon Dexter Flowers, Celeste Gurevich, Jennifer Robin, William Perkins, Jessica Poe, Anika Martin, Madison Savi Maker, Jamie Jensen, Kristel Daunell, Jessica Hanley, Emily Serb, Rachel Andrade, Aubrey Lovegrove, Kevin Shamel, Kristen Graetz, Juliet Escoria, Gabino Iglesias, Cody Goodfellow, Charles Mentken, Bili Zehner, Erica Ryberg, Tim Holtom, Robert Bina, the Bizarro Community, anyone who has supported Ladybox/its authors/me/my words/ my family/given me a place to read or be read, and all the dogs I've ever met or gawked at on the internet. Thank you.

About the Author

Constance Ann Fitzgerald is the editor/curator of Ladybox Books, a zine maker, and author of the Bizarro novella *Trashland A Go-Go*. She grew up in central Arizona and has spent the last decade crawling the northwest. She currently resides in Portland, Oregon, where her happiness is wholly contingent upon whether or not there is a dog in the room.